Defensive Play

A BOYS ON THE BRINK NOVELLA

JAMIE DEACON

Ink Lane
Publishing

Defensive Play

Published 2024 Ink Lane Publishing
First Published 2018 by Beaten Track Publishing
Copyright © 2018–2024 Jamie Deacon

Paperback ISBN: 978 1 0686249 2 6
eBook ISBN: 978 1 0686249 3 3

Cover Design: Natasha Snow
www.natashasnow.com

Editing and Formatting: Debbie McGowan
www.inroadpublishing.com

To all of you who have ever felt the need to hide away, afraid of revealing the person you are inside, this one's for you.

CHAPTER ONE

I'M WALKING ONTO the football pitch with the rest of my team when I see him.

I stumble to a halt, boots skidding on the water-logged ground, and squint through the rain. Even surrounded by his teammates, all decked out in their royal blue and yellow, he draws my gaze. There's something barely suppressed about him—the way he's never still, shifting from foot to foot, his stocky frame vibrating with a restless energy. The boy must be new. He wasn't playing for the Buzzards when we came up against them last season. I'd remember.

I should look away. If anyone catches me... *Come on, Davey, get a grip.* But once I start staring, I can't stop, entranced by the muscular hardness of his thighs; the nut-brown hair plastered to his head; his shirt, drenched with rain and sweat, adhering to sculpted abs.

And then he looks at me.

The realisation slams into my stomach with the force of a penalty kick. Mud glues my studs to the touchline. I can't move, can hardly breathe. There's nothing accidental in that look. His eyes travel up my body, slow, deliberate, before connecting with mine.

The air lodges in my chest. This can't be happening. Guys like me—geeky, socially awkward—rarely attract attention, other than to provide the butt for the occasional joke. If not for my spot on the school football team, the majority of my classmates would be unaware I exist. So there's no way this boy can be looking at me—not unless...

Shit.

I avert my gaze so violently I crick my neck. Panic squeezes my heart. Have I given myself away? I must have done. Why else would he be staring at me? *Shit, shit, shit.*

"Tomkins, are you taking part in this match or have you decided to referee today?"

The voice of our coach, Mr. Barry, pulls me from my thoughts. My surroundings snap back into focus—the afternoon gloom, the sodden grass beneath my boots, the drizzle soaking into my kit and running down my exposed skin. Spectators flank the pitch—parents and siblings of the players mingling with assorted members of the teams that have already been knocked out. They grumble amongst themselves, sheltered beneath umbrellas and drawn-up hoods, and the combined weight of their impatience bears down on me.

The Brookshire football tournament is held every October at the Brookminster sports centre, with teams from sixth-forms across the county competing for a chosen charity. The first matches kicked off at ten, and by now, most people are casting longing glances in the direction of the clubhouse. I don't blame them; what I wouldn't give for a hot shower and a steaming mug of coffee.

Not that there's much prospect of either of those things for a while. My team, the Farnstead Falcons, are about to face our biggest rivals, the Brookminster Buzzards, in the second semi-final, and everyone is in position. Everyone except me.

My cheeks flame. Being caught checking out another guy is bad enough without embarrassing myself further. Thank God my parents work at weekends and aren't here to witness my humiliation. Someone sniggers behind me, but I keep my head down and jog across the field to take up my position at left back.

"All right, man?" asks Jermain Johnson, team captain and central defender for the Falcons. His bulk is enough to intimidate most players lining up a shot on goal, but he's actually a real gentle giant and always takes my side when the others give me a hard time.

I nod, unable to speak around the anxiety crushing my windpipe. I risk a peek from the corner of my eye. The boy has crouched to re-tie his laces and is no longer looking at me, but a few of his fellow players are in a huddle, talking in low voices. As I watch, one of them says something that has them doubled up with laughter. My gut twists. They're laughing at me; I know it with a certainty that has sweat breaking out on my palms. They noticed me gawping at their teammate and put two and two together. Soon the news will spread to the rest of the Buzzards, and after that it's only a matter of time before it reaches my own team.

My head swims. It's a struggle to catch my breath. I try to take it easy, to remember everything Liz taught me. Soon after I turned fourteen, when the social anxiety was at its worst, my parents persuaded me to see a cognitive behavioural therapist. Three years later, the panic attacks are still there, ready to pounce at inappropriate moments—right before a semi-final, for instance—but during those weekly sessions, I at least learned to manage them better. If not for the hours spent in Liz's office, its walls obscured behind photos of her five Staffordshire bull terriers, I would never have had the guts to try out for the Falcons.

With a huge effort, I tune out the pre-match buzz and concentrate on taking several deep breaths. In through the nose, hold for two seconds, out through the mouth. Inhale…hold… release. Inhale…hold…release. Gradually, my racing heart slows. *Just because a few of the boy's teammates were laughing*, the rational part of my brain reasons, *it doesn't automatically mean they were laughing at you. There's any number of things they could have been laughing about: a private joke, or how they were going to walk their way into the final. As for you being clocked staring too long at another guy, everyone's probably far too focused on the impending game to notice.*

"Saw you eyeing up the Buzzards' new striker," Jermain says.

I choke on my lungful of air and gape at him, powerless to hide the guilt that must be etched on my face.

"Yeah," Jermain continues, "was chatting to their captain earlier. Adam only started at Brookminster Grammar in September, but he's already their star player. Very quick. I told him we're more than a match for him."

I try to smile, but my muscles won't cooperate. Adam. So that's his name, the name of this boy who holds my secret in his hands.

In a distant recess of my brain, I hear the whistle blow. The spectators bellow in approval, their shouts rising above the smack of leather on leather. It's electric. On any other day, the atmosphere would have galvanised me, transforming me from the chemistry nerd who does practice exam papers to relax, into a confident sportsman, sure of my ability to handle the ball.

Being slight and wiry, I don't have the typical build for a defender. As a result, players often underestimate me…to their cost. I might not look like much, but I'm fast. At least, I am normally. Right now, wherever my head is, it definitely isn't in the game.

"Davey, where the fuck were you?" Kyle Matthews, our goalkeeper, glares at me, having been forced to come off his line to boot the ball to safety, a ball I should have dealt with.

I mouth an apology and make a valiant attempt to focus, but as I survey the pitch, following the sequence of play, I see him again—Adam. He has the ball, moving with it as though it's an extension of his body. I can't help it. I take in his legs, sturdy and strong and corded with muscle. Jermain wasn't exaggerating; the guy's quick. Stu Willis, our best defensive midfielder, goes in with a tackle, but Adam weaves around him with ease.

And charges right at me.

Shock cements me in place. I forget where I am, what I'm doing here. Up closer, I can make out the boy's eyes, almost the same blue as his shirt, sparkling with mischief. Adam smiles at me, a wicked smile full of challenge, daring me to stop him.

"Don't just stand there like a lemon, Tomkins. Show him what you're made of!"

Coach's agonised roar spurs me into action. Adam is almost on top of me. In my periphery, I spy Jermain tracking back to cover me, but it's too late. Only I can intercept him. Desperate to redeem myself for my poor performance, I go in hard. Too hard. My foot misses the ball entirely and clips Adam's ankle, sending him sprawling.

The referee's whistle cuts through the outraged cries from the Buzzards' supporters. I don't wait to be shown the red card.

I hesitate just long enough to watch Adam scramble to his feet, reassuring myself he's all right, and then I'm running.

"Oy, Tomkins!" Coach calls after me as I sprint past him. "This match isn't finished."

Ignoring him, deaf to the angry muttering from the spectators, I make a dash for it, across the field and around the side of the clubhouse. I need to get away, to be somewhere quiet, somewhere I can think.

In the shower block, I shove open the heavy door to one of the changing rooms and let it bang shut behind me, muting the sounds from the game. Only the clunking and groaning of an antique radiator breaks the silence. Not that it's having much effect on the temperature; it's almost as dingy and cold inside as it is out. Distantly, I remember the tracksuit I've left on the touchline. It doesn't matter. Though I'm shivering, my body is on fire. I glimpse my reflection in the grimy mirror hanging beside the door. Hair clings in dark strands to my forehead, and my cheeks are flushed, my eyes too bright. I look feverish, scared.

I collapse onto one of the benches and lean against the metal locker behind it, covering my face with my hands. My heart hammers against my ribs as though I've narrowly escaped an attacker. I inhale, telling myself to calm down. Anyone would think I've never had a strong reaction to a boy before. Stupid, seeing as I've known I'm attracted to guys since I understood what it means to fancy someone. This is nothing new, except…

He looked at me.

My breathing threatens to get out of control again. In all the years I've been checking out guys, staring without appearing to stare, no one has ever stared back. Never. And yet there was no mistaking the deliberate way Adam's eyes met mine. He'd seen straight through me, homing in on the desires I've been so careful to keep hidden. And if Adam saw it, who's to say he's the only one? And if he isn't, how long before the rumours start?

Nausea claws at my throat. I've never been popular; the social anxiety hinders my efforts to make friends. It was only a couple of years ago, when my therapist convinced me to pursue my passion for football and I earned my place on the team, that I'd been accepted. The Falcons are all I have, and if any of them ever found out the truth, it would be the end of everything.

Yet, even as I sit here, gut churning, I'm aware of another emotion. It's faint, almost drowned by the fear and the dread, but it's there—something unfamiliar, exciting. The seconds leading up to my sending-off replay in my mind—Adam's brilliant eyes snaring mine, the way he smiled at me. There had been no mockery in that smile, no disgust. It felt a lot like—my brain scrambles for the right word—like a promise.

There's due to be a presentation after the tournament when the trophies will be awarded, followed by a party for the players. He'll be there—Adam. The thought of seeing him again, of maybe even talking to him, ties my stomach in knots. I can't go; I so nearly gave myself away during the match. Being in the same room as Adam is a risk I can't afford to take. It would be foolhardy, dangerous. I have too much to lose.

CHAPTER TWO

"So what happened out there?" Jermain flops into the chair beside mine.

It's the second time I've been asked this in as many hours. After the tournament, once the players had showered and changed and were heading over to the clubhouse for the presentation, Mr. Barry held me back. He waited until we were alone in the changing room before rounding on me.

"What the hell happened?" His already ruddy face reddened further with anger and his greying eyebrows met in a scowl.

Head bowed, I stared at a crack dissecting the tile under my foot. What could I say?

"Well? What got into you? Could've done that boy a serious injury."

My face burned. It was true. All Adam did was smile at me, and I'd nearly broken his ankle. "I'm sorry. I…didn't feel too good. Wasn't concentrating."

"Weren't concentrating? I'm telling you, Tomkins, if that had been an important match…"

Coach didn't need to finish the threat. Not only had the tackle been dangerous, it had cost us the semi-final, assisting the Buzzards to a 4-1 victory. Had it taken place during a cup game, I could have been suspended, and deservedly so.

Mr. Barry laid a hand on my shoulder. "Listen, I know you didn't do it on purpose. Next time you're unfit, tell me, all right? I'd rather have to sub you than play with ten men."

I chanced a look at him. His expression, though still stern, had softened a fraction. Coach can be pretty tough on his players, but only because he wants to get the best out of us.

Two hours later, in the face of Jermain's concern, I drop my head in my hands. "I'm so sorry. I seriously messed up."

"Don't sweat it, man. Could've happened to anyone."

"The others don't see it like that. You heard what they were saying after the match, and they're right. It's my fault we got slaughtered."

"Nah." Jermain punches my shoulder. "They were just screwing with you. You know what they're like. You OK, though? You went kind of weird on us."

"I felt weird, but I'm better now."

It isn't a lie—not entirely. I'm still jittery, hyperaware of my body, as if there's a live current running through my nerve endings, but that initial blinding panic has receded. When my team joined me in the shower block—thankfully the Buzzards weren't sharing our changing room—all they could talk about was the tackle and how I'd handed Brookminster the final on a plate. There was nothing about Adam, about whatever had passed between us. Perhaps I really have got away with it.

So, here I am, skulking in a dark corner of the clubhouse and trying not to be noticed. After the presentation, the families went home and the players' girlfriends arrived. The party's in full throttle, dance music blasting from the stereo. The teams from the various schools mingle indiscriminately, the on-field rivalry of a few hours earlier replaced by the camaraderie of the game.

I shouldn't be here. I had to show for the presentation or I would've looked like a total sore loser, but I hadn't meant to stay. I'd promised myself, as soon as the trophies were handed out, I'd slip away. I also made a pact not to stare at Adam when, inevitably, he went up to collect his award for player of the tournament. I'd meant it, too. I just couldn't help myself.

While Jermain talks, giving a blow-by-blow account of the match following the red card, my attention slides inexorably to the far side of the room. It doesn't matter that the clubhouse is packed; I have no trouble picking him out. Off the pitch, I'm Mr. Invisible, the one girls shove past to reach the more popular boys. Adam, however, is a magnet for admiration. There's an aura about him, a charisma, that has a whole group jostling around him like he's Harry Cain. I even spot a few Falcons among his fans.

The strange thing is, he manages it without being loud or in your face. Adam's obviously the centre of the gathering, and yet, as far as I can tell, he's not saying all that much. He laughs a lot, the infectious sound drifting over the general hubbub, and occasionally he'll toss in a comment that has the guys creasing up. Mostly, though, he shifts with that same restlessness I observed earlier, his eyes sweeping the room as if searching for something.

Or someone.

It happens again; Adam's gaze snags mine. A jolt that's part excitement, part apprehension, shoots through me. I thought I was safe, tucked away in my corner, but somehow, perhaps sensing the heat of my scrutiny, Adam found me. And he's caught me staring...again.

I wrench my eyes away and press a palm to my forehead. All at once the room feels too hot, too claustrophobic. I'm so lost in my own mortification that when Jermain touches my shoulder, I jump.

"Easy," he says. "Sure you're all right? You're burning up."

I take a deep breath and push my chair back. I need to get out of here before I make a complete idiot of myself. "Going to get some air."

"Want me to come with you?"

"No, you're fine. See you in a bit."

I grab my Falcons hoodie from the back of my chair, then push my way through the crowd and out of the front entrance.

The rain has stopped. A soft mist hangs in the air, turning the distant streetlights a hazy orange. After the stuffiness of the clubhouse, the night is bitterly cold, and I pull on my hoodie against the chill. I sit on the steps overlooking the car park, heedless of the damp that seeps through my jeans. Elbows on knees, I rest my chin in my hands and close my eyes, attempting to clear my mind. I don't want to think anymore. I just want to sit with nothing but the dark and the quiet for company.

I haven't been hunched there long when the door opens, ejecting a stream of warmth and thumping bass. I glance behind me, although I know who it will be. My body goes still. Adam lets the door swing shut and, just like that, we're alone.

He doesn't seem surprised to find me on the steps. Perhaps he saw me leave. Has he followed me? My insides clench. What if Adam thinks I did it deliberately, that I meant to lure him out here. Maybe I had. Maybe, deep down, a part of me hoped Adam might come, even while the rest of me prayed he wouldn't.

This time, when our gazes connect, there's no one to see, no football match to act as a buffer. I drink him in. Even in the faint glow filtering through the frosted pane in the door, his eyes are a vivid blue.

"Hey," Adam says. Such a simple word that expresses so much. There's recognition there, like we're childhood friends meeting after years apart, but uncertainty, too. He has a nice voice, I register through my turbulent thoughts—warm and slightly husky.

"Hey." My reply emerges somewhere between a croak and a squeak. Cringing, I stare down at my feet.

"It's Davey, right?"

I fling him a startled look. Has this boy—this confident, gorgeous boy—actually gone to the trouble of finding out my name?

One side of Adam's mouth lifts in a crooked smile. "Well, I had to know who the lunatic was who almost took my leg off."

"God." I bury my face in my hands. Of course Adam was going to ask about me after what happened on the pitch. "I'm so sorry."

He laughs and nudges my thigh with the toe of his trainer. "I'm kidding. Seriously, you did us a favour."

I dare a peep at him, unable to rid myself of the thought that he has pursued me out here to take the piss. That wouldn't be anything new, after all.

"It's true." Adam crouches on the step beside me, his expression amused but without malice. "Rob warned me about you. He said the rest of your defence is pretty solid but probably not quick enough to catch me. You were the real threat."

I grimace. "I'm guessing he wasn't expecting me to take you out quite so spectacularly, though."

"Funnily enough, that wasn't included in the pep talk. Still, I should be thanking you. You made our job a whole lot easier."

"Don't remind me. You should've heard the guys after the match. I'll never hear the end of it."

Adam laughs again, and I can't hold back a smile. Here I am, having an actual conversation with an amazing-looking boy—a boy who'd caught me checking him out, no less—and I'm not making an ass of myself.

The door behind us bursts open and several guys spill out. I tense, guard raised. Will they think it odd us sitting out here alone? I scan their faces, but none are from Farnstead. A moment later, they barrel down the steps without giving either of us a second glance and head for one of the cars parked nearby.

As they pile in and the engine growls to life, I exhale, shoulders slumping. I sense Adam studying me and keep my gaze lowered.

"You're not out," he says, "are you?"

"What?" My entire body goes rigid. He knows. I'd already guessed as much, but suspecting it is one thing; being confronted with the indisputable truth sends me spiralling back into panic mode. Why had he really followed me out here? I'd thought... been sure I'd read something in his eyes when they locked with mine, but what if I'm wrong? Do I truly believe someone like Adam, someone popular and self-assured, would have sought me out? Unless...

In my mind, I see again the Brookminster players in their huddle, sniggering, moments after Adam caught me staring. I'd reassured myself they weren't laughing about me, but perhaps my fears had been well founded. The cold certainty settles like a snowball in my gut. I'd given myself away, and now the other lads have sent Adam out here to chat me up, trick me into an admission I won't be able to take back. For all I know, his mates are somewhere close by as we speak, listening in.

"Hey." Adam extends his palms in what is probably supposed to be a calming gesture. "It's all right. I know, and it's all right."

"You don't know anything," I snap. The instinct for self-preservation, to keep my protective wall intact at any cost, propels me to my feet. "You hear me? You don't know anything about me."

Before he can respond, I'm down the steps and sprinting into the darkness, phone already out to call my parents. All I want is to go home, crawl into bed, and forget today ever happened.

CHAPTER THREE

"Davey." A gentle touch smooths my hair. "Sweetheart, time to get up."

I claw my way from the quagmire of sleep and peel my eyes open. "Huh?"

Mum's face swims into view, peering down at me. "Time to get ready for school. You slept through your alarm."

Hardly surprising, given my disturbed night. In a sickening rush, the events of the day before crash into me: the tackle, the sending off, the noisy stuffiness of the clubhouse...and Adam. Adam meeting my gaze across the field, pursuing me out onto the steps, trying to trick me with his smile and those incredible eyes.

"Everything OK?" Mum perches on the edge of the bed and lays a hand on my forehead. "Still feeling poorly?"

"Tired." My voice comes out groggy and cracked, and a dull ache throbs at my temples.

I'd collapsed into bed the moment Mum brought me home last night, only to lie awake long into the early hours. Gut churning, my muscles locked tight with apprehension, I relived over and over how close I came to dropping my guard, to losing everything.

"Perhaps you should stay home today." Mum scans my face. Her eyes, the same shade of espresso as my own, are shadowed with concern. No trophy for guessing who I inherited my anxiety from, although hers is less acute, more general.

I consider it—just for a second. It would be so easy to give in, to burrow back under the covers and hide from the world a little longer. On another day, I might have done. It wouldn't be the first time I've played up the symptoms of my anxiety, begging to be allowed to stay home—anything other than endure the daily torture of interacting with my classmates. I haven't resorted to this so much lately, though. Not since Liz helped me manage things; not now I have the Falcons.

Had the Falcons.

My stomach twists. The fact is, I have no idea what will be waiting for me at school, how many of my own teammates were in on Adam's ruse.

You didn't admit to anything, I tell myself. *You didn't do anything at all that could be seen as incriminating.*

Except run away, a snide voice whispers in my ear, and if that isn't a confession of guilt, I don't know what is.

"Davey?" Mum's still studying me, no doubt searching for signs of whatever illness drove me home early from the party.

"I can't." The words sit heavy on my tongue. "Have a mock chemistry exam."

"Well, if you're sure you're up to it."

I'm not sure of anything save for the familiar queasiness rolling around in my stomach, but the mocks are important, a chance to have a crack at a past A' Level paper in real exam conditions. I can't afford to miss it, however much I might want to stay cocooned in the safety of my bedroom. So I give Mum what I hope is a reassuring smile and drag myself out of bed to face the day.

DO THEY KNOW?

As we file into the assembly hall, which has been transformed into an exam room by banks of desks and uncomfortable-looking wooden chairs, I steal furtive peeps at my A' Level chemistry class. Has the news reached them yet? I'm the only member of the Falcons taking this subject, so it's possible no one has heard. On the other hand, Lucy Rogers went out with Kyle for most of Year Eleven, and they're still part of the same crowd…

Heart pounding, light-headed with apprehension, I slide into my assigned seat in the third row. I hunch over, braced for the onslaught of sniggers and whispered insults, but everyone seems far too busy sharpening pencils and biting their fingernails to pay me any attention. Either the gossip hasn't had a chance to spread, or exam nerves have pushed any rumours about me to the backs of their minds.

"OK, settle down." Mrs. Simpson moves between the desks, handing out papers.

With a jolt, I realise I've been so preoccupied with the prospect of being outed that I've forgotten to be anxious about the mock. I barely have time to check my supplies—pencils, rubber, sharpener—before Mrs. Simpson returns to the front and instructs us to begin.

A hush falls over the hall, broken only by pages rustling and the scratching of pencils. As I turn my paper over and read the first question, everything else fades away. I lose myself in acids and alkalis, elements and formulae, their safe predictability soothing me as they never fail to do.

LATER, I STAND under the shower in the school changing room, face tilted up to the spray, my eyes closed. The water—never quite hot enough however high you crank the dial—massages the aches of another tough training session and eases the tension of the past twenty-four hours.

Even if the chemistry paper hadn't calmed me, the behaviour of my teammates would have. Nothing in their attitude during practice suggested they saw me any differently. Jermain greeted me with concern, wanting to know where I'd disappeared to last night, while the others continued to rib me about yesterday's red card. Normally, the teasing would have got to me, but not today. Today I was glad of it—welcomed it, even. The harmless banter was the proof I needed that I'm still one of the team, that the Falcons weren't in league with Adam.

Mr. Barry held me back after practice to check I'm fit to play against Oakbridge on Friday. By the time I made it to the changing room, my teammates were in various stages of dress; I have the showers to myself.

I linger under the spray, listening to the shouted goodbyes and the banging of the swing door as the room empties. After years of sharing changing rooms with my teammates, I'm used to being surrounded by a dozen naked guys, if not entirely immune to it. All the same, I live in constant fear that a careless glance, an accidental straying of eyes to where they're not supposed to be, will betray me, and so I tend to dawdle in the shower, allowing the others to cover up.

Judging by the noise level beyond the shower curtain, all but a couple of the guys have left. I reach for the shower gel and squeeze a glob into my hands, their words filtering to me through the trickle of running water.

"You're winding me up, right?" Kyle's voice, full of incredulity, bounces off the tiled walls.

Stu, Kyle's best mate, answers, "That's what Mark Henderson told me. I was chatting to him yesterday at the party. He's not likely to make something like that up, is he?"

I go still. Mark Henderson plays midfield for Brookminster, and, thinking back, I'm certain he was one of the Buzzards I'd seen laughing before the semi-final. I'd noticed him and Stu talking last night but hadn't thought anything of it. How could I have been so complacent? My breathing accelerates; I can't draw enough air into my lungs. It's as though all the oxygen has been sucked from the shower cubicle. They know. Mark must have told Stu at the party, and now Stu has filled Kyle in.

Kyle lets out a snort of disgust. "And he's still on the team? Why the hell didn't they give the poofter the boot?"

"Why do you think? You saw how he plays, how fast he is. He took our defence to pieces. Once Davey got sent off, we didn't stand a chance."

My mouth drops open. Water drips from my fringe into my eyes, but I make no move to wipe it away. They're not talking about me. I should feel relieved, but I don't. Realisation oozes through my veins, tinged with the prickling heat of shame.

"Good on Davey," Kyle says. "Wish I'd brought the pansy down myself."

Stu laughs. "Yeah, never knew Davey had it in him. That was one serious tackle."

"Served him right. I don't care how quick he is. He shouldn't be allowed on the pitch. You wouldn't catch me playing on the same team as a homo."

"The games would be the least of your worries, I reckon. Mark said their coach makes them share a changing room with him. That Adam must think he's in heaven every time they strip off."

"That's sick." There's a clunk as though Kyle has thrown something at the metal lockers. "No way I'd have some poof checking out my arse."

My head spins. Bile burns the back of my throat. Sometimes, lying awake in the lonely hours, I've wondered what would happen if I plucked up the courage to come out. It all plays out in my mind—the disappointment, the disgust—but the reality of it, hearing with my own ears the mockery in Stu's tone, the vehement hatred in Kyle's, is so much worse than I ever imagined.

I reach out to steady myself against the tiles, legs threatening to crumple beneath me. My elbow knocks the bottle of shower gel, which falls to the floor with a clatter.

"Oy, Davey." The shower curtain is ripped aside, revealing Kyle's smirking face. "You jerking off in there?"

Heat roars through my body. I stare at him, exposed and vulnerable, my brain too full of confusion to conjure up a reply.

Stu sniggers. "I know you lost us the tournament yesterday, Davey, but there's no need to try and drown yourself."

"Yeah, don't beat yourself up over it," Kyle says. "You gave that queer what he deserved."

With a supreme effort, I straighten my spine and lift one shoulder in what I pray passes for an offhand shrug. To distract myself from the desire to vomit, I retrieve the dropped bottle and focus on rinsing the suds from my skin.

Stu ambles into view, thumping Kyle with his sports bag as he swings it over his shoulder. "You coming?"

"Yeah." Kyle turns away. "See you, Davey."

I mumble a response, barely aware of what I'm saying, but the shower drowns my words in any case. One of them, probably Kyle, flicks the light switch before the door slams, plunging me into blackness.

I turn off the shower, fingers trembling, but make no move to reach for my towel. I simply stand there, my mind thrown into chaos, the quiet darkness broken only by the intermittent drip of water.

Adam's gay. It hadn't been a prank, him seeking me out on the clubhouse steps. Incredible as it seems, he genuinely had wanted to talk to me, spurred on by whatever had sparked between us when his gaze met mine. Adam took a chance last night, a chance on me, and I'd been too blinded by fear and suspicion to recognise the advance for what it was.

I have to talk to him.

Panic constricts my diaphragm, but the truth of what has to be done hardens like concrete in my belly. It might be too late to repair the damage, but I can't leave him with a false impression of me, can't let him believe I'm no better than people like Kyle Matthews. I only hope I have the guts to do it, and that he'll be willing to listen.

CHAPTER FOUR

A S THOUGH I'VE summoned him with the power of my thoughts, he's waiting for me when I emerge from the school building.

I'm crossing the car park to the front gates when footsteps scuff the concrete behind me. I pause, turning, and there he is—Adam. He stops no more than a few feet away, hands dug in the pockets of his battered leather jacket, a shadowy form in the darkness. What is he doing here? Can he really still want to talk to me after I made such a twat of myself yesterday, running away like a kid playing Knockdown Ginger?

Alarm jolts through me. Did any of my teammates see him? I scan our surroundings, searching for the merest sign of movement. Given what Kyle said in the changing room, I don't know how he'd react to finding Adam here, the two of us alone in the otherwise deserted car park.

"It's OK." Adam takes a hesitant step towards me, as though approaching a frightened puppy. "No one saw me. I parked over there."

I look to where he's pointing. A hunched shape crouches in the far corner, shrouded by the deeper blackness of the trees beyond the chain-link fence.

"See? No need to worry," Adam says, his tone reassuring. It's clear he thinks I'm afraid for myself, of being spied with him, and I am, but not nearly as scared as I am for him.

My gaze drops to my feet. "That isn't... I didn't mean... Sorry."

"What have you got to be sorry for?" He sounds perplexed.

"Yesterday. The way I ran out on you. I thought..." But how can I tell this boy, who has gone to such efforts to talk to me, that I'd suspected him of trying to out me for a laugh?

"Shit." Adam huffs out a long breath. "I'm the one who should be apologising."

I raise my head, startled. "Huh?"

"Well, obviously. I was an idiot. I saw how edgy you were. I should've explained. Walk with me?"

I should refuse. I've already delayed too long after practice, agonising over my decision to speak to Adam, and my parents will be expecting me home. Yet, despite the nerves knotting my insides, I don't want to. I'm drawn to this boy with his husky voice and easy friendliness, overwhelmed by the need to spend just a few moments more in his company, to hear whatever it is he came here to say.

By way of answer, I turn and head for the school gates, Adam falling into step beside me. We cross the road, busy with rush hour traffic, and start along the street. Warm light spills from a few windows, their curtains not yet drawn, throwing rectangles of amber into the darkness. Beyond that, the only illumination comes from the streetlights and the blur of passing headlamps.

"Yesterday," Adam says after a while, "when I came out to talk to you, I made a right mess of things."

I grimace. "At least you didn't do a runner."

"You were protecting yourself." One side of his mouth quirks in a crooked smile. "You didn't trust me, and why should you? You don't know me from, well, Adam."

A laugh bubbles out of me, as much from surprise as amusement, catching me off guard. I barely recognise the sound as my own.

Adam's grin widens and his eyes dance. "Yeah, coming straight out like that and asking you what I did wasn't the smartest idea I've ever had. I should've told you about myself first, so here goes. I'm Adam, I'm a striker for the Brookminster Buzzards, and I'm gay. What's more, everyone knows it."

The mirth dies in my throat. I look away. "I overheard some of my team talking about it, about you, this evening after practice."

"So my fame has spread already. That didn't take long."

He's so casual about it, so utterly self-assured in his own skin. I can't begin to wrap my mind around it. "And your team's cool with that?"

"Not all of them. When I came out, some wanted me off the squad, said they wouldn't shower in the same room as me." Adam rolls his eyes. "But my captain stuck by me, and a lot of the others did, too. I'd played several matches for the Buzzards by then, so no one could say I hadn't earned my place."

"They seem to have accepted you pretty well." I'm recalling the scene in the clubhouse, Adam surrounded by a cluster of admirers.

He shrugs. "More or less. A few of the guys still give me a hard time, but that's their problem."

We fall quiet. The constant whoosh of traffic drowns our footsteps and the thudding of my heart. I try to imagine coming out to my own team. Would the Falcons accept me the way the Buzzards have accepted Adam? Unlikely.

"It's different for you. You're popular, the sort of person everyone likes. They'd like you whatever you were. Me, though…

the guys tolerate me because I'm on the team, but that's it. I'm not…" I trail off in confusion.

Adam touches my arm, drawing me to a stop. The contact is brief, the merest graze of fingers against my sleeve. Nevertheless, it burns through the material of my sweatshirt, making my skin tingle.

"This is all kind of new to me, too," he says, "this coming out thing. My best mate at my last school knew, but no one else."

I bite my lip. A hollowness eats into my stomach. Beyond my parents, I don't have anyone I'm that close to. No one I can confide in. No one to make me feel just a little less alone. "So, what made you decide to do it now?"

"Got sick of pretending, I suppose. Being popular doesn't mean much when nobody knows who you really are. When I moved to Brookminster over the summer, I saw it as my chance. New city, new school, new people. It was a fresh start."

We begin walking again, rounding the corner onto a quieter street. What's going on in Adam's head? He must think I'm a coward for denying who I am. He probably regrets seeking me out at the clubhouse and wouldn't be here now if he hadn't felt the need to apologise.

Adam pauses in the pool of blackness between two streetlights. I linger beside him, awkward and unsure. Perhaps I should make an excuse and leave, save Adam the trouble of giving me the brush-off.

"Look," he says, "I'm not about to out you or anything, if that's what you're thinking."

I dart him a wary glance.

"No, really, I wouldn't do that. It's, well, it's personal. Outing someone without their permission is a crappy thing to do. You have to be ready, and no one gets to decide that other than you."

"It's OK, I get it. You came to apologise." I smile, but there's a strange ache in my gut. He's nice, Adam, genuinely nice. If things had played out differently at the clubhouse, if I had stayed and talked to him rather than showing myself up to be the pathetic closet case I am, maybe I could have had the opportunity to get to know him better.

"No, that isn't it. I mean, yeah, I wanted to say I was sorry, but that's not the only reason I came." Adam kicks his heel against the garden wall behind him. "I wanted to talk to you, to see if maybe you fancied getting together some time."

Heat rushes to my face. I pray it's too dark for Adam to see me blush. Have I just been asked out on a date? It makes no sense. With his confidence and good looks, Adam could have any guy he chooses.

"Why?" I ask.

"Huh?"

"Well, look at me. I'm nothing special, just a nerd who happens to play football. You must have more interesting people to spend time with."

Adam stares at me, forehead creased. "You kidding?"

I shake my head. Misery closes around my heart. Why do I have to turn a simple invitation to hang out into a big deal? Instead of saying 'sounds great, thanks', like any normal person, I have to go and ruin everything…again.

"You have no idea, do you? You honestly have no idea how sexy you are."

I snort. I'm many things—geeky, socially inept, incapable of carrying on a conversation with a hot guy without making a prat of myself—but sexy isn't one of them.

"I'm serious." Adam steps closer until he's standing right in front of me. The heat from his body mingles with mine and my pulse skyrockets. "There you were, this killer defender, all compact speed and soulful eyes, part of the team but separate from it at the same time. Then, in the clubhouse, you kept yourself to yourself, watching everything around you while trying not to be noticed. Still, every time I looked at you, saw you looking back, there was something there. You're intriguing. Can you blame me for wanting to get to know you?"

I gape at him. So much for being Mr. Invisible. But sexy? Intriguing? These are the last adjectives I would ever have applied to myself.

Adam lays a hand on my shoulder, sending a hundred volts sparking along my arm. "There's no pressure. We could order pizza, watch a film, just hang out, maybe go for a bike ride… whatever. That's if you'd like to."

For the first time, he sounds unsure of himself, and this, more than anything else, gives me courage. It will be risky. If Adam's sexuality is common knowledge, and if I'm known to be spending time with him, someone's bound to make the connection sooner or later.

All the same, I want to. I want to get to know this boy with the infectious laugh and incredible eyes. I want to be with him, to explore the connection we'd forged across a muddy field on a rainy autumn afternoon.

"Yeah," I manage through the dryness in my throat, "I'd like to."

CHAPTER FIVE

"DAVEY, ARE YOU with us?"

Though gentle as always, Mum's voice jerks me from my thoughts. I look up from the chicken and ham pie I've barely touched to find three pairs of eyes studying me with varying degrees of amusement and concern.

Thursday is family night in the Tomkins household. It's early closing day for The Tea Cosy, the small but popular tea room in Farnstead High Street owned and run by my parents, and it's the one evening we all sit around the kitchen table together. Everyone is expected to be there—no excuses.

I grimace at Mum in apology. "Did you say something?"

She nods across the table towards Dad. "Your father asked you a question, but you were away with the fairies."

I drop my fork with a clang. I retrieve it, a guilty flush swamping my cheeks. *It's an expression*—I try to calm my racing pulse—*just an expression*. Mum can't read minds. She has no way of knowing that, for the past seventy-two hours, I've been fixated on Adam…the brilliant blue of his eyes, his warm smile, the prospect of seeing him this weekend. Always assuming I can pluck up the courage to ask my sister for the much needed favour, and providing she agrees. I push the peas around my plate, my insides squirming.

Opposite me, Elle smirks into her glass of apple juice. I kick her under the table, then wince when she kicks me back twice as hard. At fourteen, my sister has inherited none of my shyness

28

and, as far as I can tell, was put on this planet solely to torment me.

"Sorry, Dad," I say, turning to him, "what was that?"

His eyes twinkle. "I wondered who you're playing tomorrow, that's all."

Dad's far more at home in The Tea Cosy's kitchen, baking scones and Victoria sponges, than he ever could be on the touchline. However many times he's asked me to explain the offside rule, he remains clueless. Still, he tries; he and Mum both do. Although work means they rarely get to see me in action, they follow the Falcons' progress in the league with the unswerving enthusiasm of true supporters.

"Oakbridge Ospreys," I tell him.

"Ah. You beat them last time, if I remember rightly."

"Three-one, yeah. Jimmy scored a hat trick."

"We'll keep our fingers crossed for another victory tomorrow then, right, girls?"

Elle, who never bothers to hide her boredom concerning all things football, opens her mouth in an exaggerated yawn.

"That could make kneading dough a little tricky." Mum smiles at Dad, then her anxious gaze returns to me. "Aren't you hungry, sweetheart?"

"Oh, yeah." I swallow a forkful of pie with an effort, the pastry joining the nerves already heavy in my stomach. *Just do it, Davey. Stop making this such a big deal.* Except, it is a big deal and my family will know it.

Mum shifts nearer to peer into my face. "You haven't had much appetite since Sunday. Are you still feeling under the weather?"

"No, really, I'm fine." My voice cracks on the lie. Given my current turmoil and my tendency to veer in an instant from excitement to raging panic, it's doubtful whether I've ever been less fine. I take a gulp of water and clear my throat. I can do this. "Um, Elle, can I ask a favour?"

"What sort of favour?" My sister's eyes, green like Dad's but infinitely more piercing, narrow with suspicion.

"Nothing important. If you can't, it really doesn't matter. I just…could we swap shifts this weekend?"

Elle gapes at me as though I've broken into operatic song. Thinking about it, she'd probably find my tone deafness blossoming into a Pavarotti tenor at the dinner table less startling. My sister bagged the Sunday shift as soon as she was old enough to help out at The Tea Cosy, arguing that, since I had less of a social life than she does, working Saturdays wouldn't matter so much. I've never minded; it isn't as if I've had anything better to do…until now.

"Why?" Elle asks, mistrust stretching the question into several syllables.

"I'm, uh, going out with someone. A friend." The inevitable blush creeps up my neck, and I pretend to be intent on cutting off a sliver of pie. God, had I made that sound like a date? Well, it is a date, kind of, but I hadn't wanted to advertise the fact.

"You don't have any friends," Elle says with her usual bluntness.

"Danielle, that's unkind," Mum chides. "Who is this friend, Davey?"

Even focused on my plate, I can feel my family watching me, interested, expectant, and my reply comes out in a nervous rush. "Adam. We…we met at the tournament last weekend. He asked if I wanted to hang out on Saturday, since he has practice on Sunday. Don't worry, Elle, if you already have plans. It's no big deal. Just a bike ride and maybe a pizza afterwards. We can always do it another time."

I trail off into mortified silence, resisting the urge to sink my burning face in my hands. Please, someone, rip out my tongue and prevent me from speaking ever again. Could I have sounded any more guilty and desperate if I tried?

"Ooh!" Elle's lips curve in an evil grin. "Davey has a boy—"

"Shut up." My furious hiss cuts her off before she can finish. I know she's winding me up, that I shouldn't rise, but the boyfriend taunt comes far closer to the truth than anyone but me realises.

"What?" Her tone drips innocent affront. "I was only saying—"

Dad silences her with a frown. "Give your brother a break, eh?"

I shoot him a grateful look. It isn't that I think my family would have a problem with me being gay. Elle would take the piss—nothing new there—but I'm sure my parents would be supportive, just as they are with my football. All the same, they worry about me enough already, what with the anxiety and my difficulty making friends. The last thing I want is to add to that.

"Well, I think it's lovely you have someone to go out with." Mum beams at me. She doesn't say 'at last', but I hear it under the relief in her voice. "And I'm sure Elle won't mind swapping shifts this once."

My sister shrugs. "Whatever. I'm not doing anything that day. Besides, who am I to stand in the way of Davey's love li— hey!"

I throw a slice of carrot at her, and she ducks, laughing.

"Go Falcons," Kyle whoops, punching the air. "Two-nil. Two fucking nil! Top of the league, here we come."

I can't stop grinning. We rush the door of the changing room, united in a tangle of elation and mud-caked limbs with me at its heart. My teammates crowd around me, high-fiving each other and slapping one another on the back.

We won!

Euphoria sings through my bloodstream, humming a victory song in my ears. Too much on a high to suffer the usual hangups over undressing in front of the guys, I peel off my sweat-soaked kit and run for the showers with everyone else. Face tilted up to the spray, I relive the highlights of the match while my teammates indulge in verbal replays and discuss their plans for the coming half-term.

Clean and refreshed, I wander back into the main changing area to dry off and pull on fresh clothes, my team still buzzing around me.

"Man, that second goal." Stu claps Jimmy on the shoulder. "You must've shot from thirty-five yards. Their goalie never saw it coming."

Jermain nudges me. "Unlike our Davey. Nothing got past him today. He played a blinder."

In the midst of pulling on my trainers, I duck my head to hide my smile, which must be as daft as anything. In contrast to my disastrous performance during the tournament, the nervous anticipation of seeing Adam tomorrow lent an extra ferocity to my game until I felt that nothing and no one could touch me.

Jimmy grins at me from the bench opposite. "Seriously, you were on fire today. Whatever you've been taking, I want some."

"Davey's in lurve," Kyle drawls.

"Wh-what?" Panic, hot and sticky, wipes the smile from my face. How does he know? Did someone see me with Adam? Have I really been that obvious?

"Ha! I knew it." Kyle hurls his sweaty football shorts at me, eyes glinting with malicious amusement. "You've been grinning like an idiot all week. Who is she?"

"Yeah, Davey, who's the lucky lady?" Stu chimes in.

Embarrassment sets my skin on fire. "I… No, it isn't… I'm not…"

But my teammates don't want to hear my denial. Voices bombard me from all sides, laughter interspersed with demands to know the identity of this mystery girl.

"Come on, Davey, give us a hint," Stu cajoles. "She must be something special. I didn't think you knew what a girl was."

Kyle smirks. "Yeah, was starting to think you were into other balls besides the punting kind."

My fingers fumble with my laces. *Don't react. If he really suspected, he wouldn't be laughing about it.* I sit there, keeping my mouth shut, and wait for the blessed moment when I can melt once more into the background.

At last, Jermain raises his voice over the hilarity. "OK, guys, give it a rest, yeah?"

They quiet down, although Jimmy winks at me whenever I catch his eye, and Kyle elbows me as he delves into the locker beside mine. I focus on shoving my dirty kit into my bag, stomach roiling, palms slick with perspiration. They were joking, giving me shit the way they would any other teammate, treating me like one of them. Only, I'm not. However hard I try to ignore it, the question echoes in my mind: how different would their reaction have been if they knew the truth?

CHAPTER SIX

I WAKE UP ON Saturday morning to the sound of torrential rain hammering against my bedroom window. I lie there for a while without opening my eyes, the anticipation that has carried me through the past week crumbling to dust. So much for the bike ride we'd planned. I'd been consumed by the prospect of spending the day with Adam, looking forward to and fretting about it in equal measure, and now the weather has spoiled it.

My phone chimes to signal an incoming text. With a speed generally reserved for the football pitch, I bolt upright and snatch it off the bedside cabinet, reading the short message from Adam.

Want to come over?

Happiness, pure and uncomplicated for once, expands in my chest. As I tap out a reply, I catch sight of myself in the mirror on the wall above the chest of drawers, scarcely recognising the goofy grin as my own.

Be there in an hour.

After a hurried shower, I pull on clean jeans and my favourite navy blue hoodie and, snatching the car keys from the telephone table, head downstairs to the rear hallway. I push open the door that leads straight into The Tea Cosy's kitchen and am immediately enveloped in sugar-scented steam. "Dad, OK if I borrow the car?"

He looks over from the counter where he's up to his forearms in dough and smiles at me. "Bike ride cancelled, then?"

"Yeah. We're, uh, going to hang out at Adam's instead." I will myself not to blush, even as the telltale heat burns my cheeks. I glance away, jingling the car keys in a show of nonchalance I'm far from feeling.

"Have fun." Dad winks at me before returning to his dough. "Don't do anything I wouldn't do."

It's a typical Dad comment—he cracks the exact same joke every time Elle goes out—but I cringe all the same. If only he knew.

"Davey, have you had breakfast?" Mum bustles in from the main tea room, a tray of dirty crockery balanced on her arms.

"Uh, yeah." The lie comes out sounding less than convincing, but I can't exactly tell her the truth: that my stomach is so knotted with nervous excitement, it spasms at the mere suggestion of food.

"Davey." Mum sighs, pronouncing my name in that reproving way she has that separates it into two distinct words. "Wait there."

"Really, I don't…" I begin, but she's already reaching for one of the freshly baked scones cooling on its metal rack.

I hover by the door, shifting from foot to foot in my impatience to be off, while Mum cuts the scone in half and slathers it with butter.

"Here you are." She wraps the scone in a napkin and presses it into my reluctant hand, her gaze apprehensive. "Now, do take care driving in this rain, won't you? The roads will be dangerous. Enjoy your day, sweetheart. Oh, and don't forget to phone if you're going to be late."

I hug her, promising to drive slower than a milk float, then make my escape before her imagination can throw up a hundred more potential hazards. In the hall, I grab my coat from its hook, thrust the scone into the pocket, and step out into the downpour.

It's only a twenty-minute drive to Brookminster, but this is more than enough time for my brain to embark on its anxious spiral. What if the whole thing is really awkward? A bike ride would have helped break the ice, provided us with something else to focus on. It would have given us a chance to get to know each other somewhere neutral, without the added pressure of family introductions. *God!* A terrifying thought occurs to me, and the first real panic I've experienced since waking up starts my fingers tingling. Will I have to meet Adam's parents? I'm bound to trip over my tongue in my nervousness, leaving them with the impression that I'm a jibbering idiot. Worst of all, and highly likely, what if a few hours in my company is enough to prove to Adam that I'm neither sexy nor intriguing, but just dull old Davey?

Adam lives in an apartment block located behind Brookminster High Street. I pull into the car park at the end of the road and unglue my palms from the steering wheel, wiping them on my jeans. I suck in a slow breath in an effort to calm my queasiness. For a few moments, I stare out of the rain-blurred windscreen. Heavy drops beat a rapid drumroll on the roof, keeping time with my pulse.

What if I were simply to restart the car and go home? I could make some excuse, tell Adam I've changed my mind about hanging out. That way, I could hold onto the promise of what might have been, the tantalising shimmer of possibility untarnished by awkwardness or disappointment. A football-sized lump of lead settles in my gut. I can't give up on this thing with Adam before it has even begun. I may well end up making a fool of myself, but I have to take that risk. I need to find out where, if anywhere, this path might lead.

I sit up straighter, resolve overcoming my anxiety, at least for now. No use waiting for the weather to let up; I'll be here all day. Throwing open the driver's door, I hurl myself into the downpour and make a mad dash across the road. A vicious wind flings the rain into my face, drenching me in seconds. With considerable relief, I duck into the porch of Adam's building, push my wet fringe out of my eyes and press the buzzer for number nine.

The lock disengages with a hum and a click, and Adam's voice crackles over the speaker, its husky warmth obvious even through the distortion. "Come on up. Second floor."

Damn, that voice. It does something weird to my stomach, makes it feel jittery and weightless, as though it's been pumped full of helium. I push the door inwards and take the stairs at a jog. My feet, so adept on the football field, suddenly feel too large for my body and seem determined to trip me up.

Adam's waiting for me in the doorway of number nine. He grins at me when I reach the landing—a wide, infectious grin—his eyes even bluer than in my memory. I smile back, shy, hopeful, and for a while, we simply stand there, beaming at each other, while I try to remember why I'd been so worried.

"Come on, then," Adam says at last, and leads me into the apartment. As he closes the door behind us, his gaze darts to my wet hair. "You look cold. Want a cup of tea? Coffee?"

"Tea would be great," I say with way more enthusiasm than is strictly necessary. I blush. *Christ, Davey, he's offering you a drink, not a Brookminster United season ticket.*

Adam laughs, a friendly sound that holds no mockery. It seems to say, *yeah, you're a dork but I like it.*

I follow him through a doorway to the right and into the galley kitchen. While Adam fills the kettle, I lean against the worktop and glance around the small space, all white gloss and granite surfaces. Unlike our kitchen, with its scratched wood and loose handles, everything here looks top of the range, straight from one of the interior design programmes my parents love to watch. Still, there's something soulless about the lack of what Mum calls 'homely touches'—no display jars of rice and pasta, no colourful tea towel hanging on the oven door. If not for the breadboard left abandoned and littered with crumbs, and the pile of dirty crockery in the sink, it would be easy to believe no one lived here.

"Sorry about the bike ride," Adam says as he puts the kettle on to boil, like the weather is somehow his fault.

I shrug. "Doesn't matter."

And it doesn't. Now that I'm here, I realise I wouldn't have minded what we did so long as I got to spend time with Adam. Nevertheless, his words bring one of my anxieties creeping back. My gaze darts around the room; I half expect figures to leap out at me from the kitchen cupboards.

"It's OK." Adam looks over from where he's tossing teabags into two mugs. "There's no one here. There's only Dad, anyway, and he's out most of the time."

Relief saps the tension from my muscles and I feel pounds lighter. "What does he do, your dad?"

"He's a history professor, teaches at the university. For as long as I can remember, he's been working on his masterpiece." Adam emphasises the last word, rolling his eyes.

"Really? What's that?"

"Oh, some book about the obscure part Brookminster has played in military history, which no one but him cares about. Spends most of his time trawling through the archives in the county libraries or travelling all over the country to pick up rare books. He'll be out all day, so we'll have the place to ourselves."

Adam's gaze meets mine, his expression alight with a transparent pleasure underlined with something darker, more intense. Excitement bubbles up like molten lava inside me. For the first time since waking up that morning, I truly give myself over to the thrill of the present, of being here with this sweet, gorgeous boy and whatever this day might bring.

CHAPTER SEVEN

WE TAKE OUR tea along a carpeted hallway, its walls bare of decoration, and past a pair of double doors. Beyond these, I glimpse black leather sofas grouped around low coffee tables, their glass tops smudged and coated with dust. Like the kitchen, the living room has a barren, neglected air, apart from the books heaped in teetering towers on every surface.

"Dad bought this place already furnished," Adam says with a fleeting glance at the nearest stack of heavy volumes. "Just as well, or I'd be sleeping on a pile of military histories." He nudges open a door at the end of the hall and steps to one side.

I move past him, catching a whiff of his scent as I squeeze by—something woody and fresh that sets my pulse racing. In contrast to the rest of the apartment, Adam's room bursts with personality. A stripy duvet is draped carelessly over the bed, and the identical posters of Brookminster United that plaster my own bedroom cover the pale-grey walls. A close-up of Gary Shepard, the handsome striker I've had a crush on since he signed for them last season, occupies centre stage.

With a leap of recognition, I head straight for the shelves above the computer desk. An extensive film collection takes up the top shelves, but on the bottom one, flanked by an array of football trophies, sits a collector's edition box set shaped like the TARDIS.

I turn to Adam, who has perched on his bed to watch me, and beam at him. "You're a Whovian."

"Through and through." He grins back. "You, too?"

I nod, face aching from the breadth of my smile. To have found a boy like Adam—sexy, funny, genuinely nice—is amazing enough. Discovering that he also shares my obsession with *Doctor Who* is like winning the Premiership, Champions' League and FA Cup rolled into one.

"Favourite Doctor?" Adam leans forward, his eyes shining. Our gazes lock, connected by a quivering thread of excitement.

"Matt Smith," I say, as though there can be no doubt, just as Adam says with equal firmness, "David Tennant."

We stare at each other, Adam looking as taken aback as I feel, and then we both double up with laughter.

"OK, I wasn't expecting that." Adam straightens, still grinning. "Matt Smith comes a close second, though, so I'll let you off."

He pats the bed beside him. Heart rate accelerating, I cross to place my mug on the bedside cabinet and lower myself onto the edge of the mattress. As I pull off my jacket, my fingers find the lump in the pocket. "Oh, I forgot. I, uh, have something for you." I extract the still-warm package and hold it out.

"Ooh." Adam accepts it and unwraps the napkin to reveal the scone. His face lights up. "You bought this for me?"

"Not exactly." I blush under his gaze. "My parents run a tea room. Mum gave me this to eat on the way, but I wasn't… I thought you might like it."

"Awesome. We'll share it." Adam passes me one half before biting into the other. "Mmm."

We sit there on his bed, bodies angled towards each other, our knees not quite touching. Adam's eyes never leave my face, and I can't tear mine from his mouth, transfixed by the way he runs his tongue along his bottom lip to catch the stray crumbs. How might it feel to have that tongue curled around mine, tasting, exploring? I shift to pick up my mug, hoping to hide my flushed cheeks and the tightness in my crotch.

"That was amazing." Adam swallows the last mouthful and wipes his fingers on his jeans. "Your mum made it?"

I take a gulp of tea, scalding the roof of my mouth. "My dad. He's the real baker. Mum's better with the front-of-house stuff."

"You're a lucky bastard, you know that? I'd give anything to have my own supply of cakes. How come you're so skinny?"

"It isn't as exciting as it sounds. Mostly, we only get to eat the leftovers, and there aren't many of those, except when Dad's experimenting with a new recipe. Then my sister and I get to be his guinea pigs."

Adam reaches past me to snag his tea from the bedside cabinet, sending a jolt of electricity up my leg as his thigh brushes mine. Mug in hand, he sits back and glances at me with a half-smile. "It's crazy hearing you talk about your dad making scones and things. The closest my dad ever comes to baking is opening a packet of Jaffa Cakes. My mum, though…" He trails off, examining the contents of his mug, expression wistful.

"Where's…" I pause, curious about his mum, but wary of bringing up a topic that might be painful.

"My parents are divorced." Adam shrugs. "They split up when I was eight."

"I'm sorry."

"Don't be. Looking back, I'm amazed they stayed together as long as they did. They weren't exactly suited. Mum's pretty sociable, loves having a house full of people, whereas Dad just… isn't. Mum lives in Berkshire now, with my stepdad and younger sisters. Half-sisters, that is."

I try to imagine my own parents living apart, perhaps both married to other people, but I can't. It's impossible to picture them as anything other than two components of a well-oiled machine, each vital to the working of the other. "Do you get on with your stepdad?"

"Not particularly. We tolerate each other most of the time, but we've never been close. I've always got the impression Keith would've preferred it if Mum hadn't already had a child when he met her. He's part of the reason I decided to come and live with Dad and finish my A' Levels at Brookminster." Adam slides off the bed, setting his empty mug on the carpet and snatching up an Xbox controller. "Ready to get your arse kicked like your team did at the tournament?"

I seize Adam's pillow and throw it at him. "Bring it on."

"So, WHAT SHALL we watch?" Adam wanders over to the shelves above his desk and scans the films. "*Gangs of New York, Inception, District Nine*…?"

"Don't mind. You choose." I flop onto Adam's bed, languid from eating too much and laughing too hard. The Xbox controllers lie abandoned in the corner, beside a stack of flat cardboard boxes, bearing witness to our afternoon of pizza and *Pro Evolution Soccer*. For all its ordinariness, or maybe because of it, this has been the most amazing afternoon of my life.

He reels off some more titles, but my concentration drifts. I drink in the sight of him with his back to me—the muscles flexing beneath his sweatshirt, the jeans stretched taut over his firm arse—and imagine running my hands over those muscles, that lithe body pressed against mine.

Adam glances over his shoulder at me, a query in his expression. What had he been saying? I fumble for a response that won't give me away. "Um, yeah, that last one."

He smirks. "*Along Came Polly?*"

Talk about busted. My face grows warm. Now I can either come clean and admit I'd been too busy checking him out to pay attention, or confess to a secret passion for soppy Jennifer Anniston movies. Both seem equally embarrassing.

"Kidding." His smirk widens. "Knew you weren't listening."

"Oh, God." Mortified, I throw up an arm to shield my eyes. "Sorry."

"Who's complaining?" The teasing note has left Adam's voice. From beneath my forearm, I follow his gaze as it trails down the length of my body. It's a look that has the heat spreading from my face to every inch of me, and which makes me feel sexy, desirable, in a way I never have before.

Adam selects a film without looking and slips it into the player. The TV comes to life with the opening credits, and music fills the room, but I'm focused entirely on Adam as he crosses to stand by the bed. "Budge up."

I shift over on the single mattress, heart jackhammering in my throat, until I'm pressed against the wall. Adam flops beside me, and the springs dip under his weight so that I tilt into him. All at once there's no air in my lungs. At every point of contact—shoulders, arms, thighs—my nerves tingle, though not with the unpleasant prickling that signals the onset of an anxiety attack. This sets my skin alight with the insistent need to be touched.

The movie, something with Leonardo DiCaprio, unfolds on the screen, but I'm scarcely aware of it. My brain has dissolved, melted into a puddle of desire. I'm conscious of nothing save for the boy lying next to me, close enough that his arm caresses mine with every intake of breath.

I risk a sideways peep and find Adam's eyes on me. The expression in those eyes, an expression that mirrors everything I'm craving in this moment, has the air hitching in my chest. With infinite slowness, Adam rolls onto his side to face me. He props himself up on one elbow, his gaze exploring my face, moving from my eyes to my mouth and back again, a silent request for permission. I return his scrutiny, trying to convey to him without words all I know I want and a whole lot more I can't put a name to.

Then he kisses me.

I've daydreamed about it so often, my first kiss. I've tried to conjure up how it would feel, the pressure of another boy's mouth on mine, our tongues and saliva mingling, but as our lips meet, I realise no amount of fantasising could do justice to the reality.

Adam's mouth grazes mine, soft and warm, almost tentative. Yet even this gentle pressure sends a bolt of sensation stabbing through me, pulled by an invisible wire from my lips to my groin. I gasp, my hands moving of their own volition to glide over Adam's back, burning even through his sweatshirt. Adam echoes my gasp. He adjusts his position so that his hips are flush against mine, dragging a moan from somewhere deep in my throat.

He draws back a fraction, his breathing unsteady, and scans my face. "This OK? If I'm going too fast—"

Before he can finish the thought, I cup the back of his head and crush his mouth down on mine. Adam lets out a groan, his lips parting for my tongue. Incredible as it seems, he wants me every bit as much as I want him. The knowledge is heady, exhilarating. I tug him closer, my hands in his hair, and kiss him with a hunger that demonstrates to him in a way I could never have put into words how completely, unequivocally OK this is.

CHAPTER EIGHT

Adam and I spend every spare moment together over the following days. With it being half-term, I'd normally divide my time between homework and helping out at The Tea Cosy. My parents, however, unable to disguise how thrilled they are that their socially inept son has found a friend at last, insist I go and enjoy myself and practically shove me out of the front door each morning.

The dismal weather continues, keeping us confined to Adam's flat, but we don't mind. The hours pass in a pleasurable haze of watching films, playing on his Xbox, laughing until our stomachs hurt, kissing, touching, exploring. I can't get enough of him— of the warmth of his lips on mine, his tongue in my mouth, the burning smoothness of his skin under my hands. I want to drown in him, to sink so far inside him that I'll never find my way out.

But it's more than that, this thing between us—more than purely physical. We talk endlessly, saying whatever comes into our heads, no barriers between us. I tell Adam things only my family knows, about my anxiety, the isolation I endured before joining the Falcons, and he confides to me his fears that being openly gay will hamper his chances of playing professional football. For the first time in my life, I have a friend, a soul mate. For the first time in my life, there's another human being who truly sees me, understands who I am. It's intoxicating.

Adam's dad comes and goes in an unobtrusive sort of way. On Monday afternoon, Adam and I are throwing together a makeshift lunch from the few ingredients we've managed to unearth—dried pasta, a tin of tomatoes, some hard cheddar—when the front door clicks shut and a slight man wanders into the kitchen.

"Ah." He pauses, a stack of heavy books in his arms, blinking at us through thick spectacles. "Hello there."

My immediate thought is that Adam's dad is just how I'd imagine a professor to be—shapeless jumper worn over brown cords, hair unkempt and sticking up as though he has recently run his fingers through it. My next thought is that he looks exactly like an older, nerdier version of Adam.

"Hey, Dad." Adam glances up from his saucepan. "This is Davey."

"Hi." I pause in my task of grating the cheddar to give him a little wave. I'm still holding the block of cheese in my hand and a few crumbs drop onto the floor. I cringe, but Adam's dad doesn't appear to notice.

"Ah," he says again, his tone contemplative, as though my name is a cryptogram he's trying to decipher. He nods and gives me a vague smile.

"Want some lunch?" Adam asks. "There's plenty."

His dad peers into the saucepan where the tomatoes are bubbling away. "Thank you. I am rather hungry, now I come to think of it. Meant to have some toast before I went out, but I can't quite remember…"

He retreats into the hallway, still muttering to himself, and then the door to his study closes with a snap.

Adam rolls his eyes and prods the contents of the pan with his wooden spoon. "I swear, he'd forget to eat if I didn't remind him."

I return to grating cheese. "Does he know about…?"

"About me? Yeah, I told him last year when I came out at school."

"What did he say?"

"Not a lot. As you may have gathered, he's not much of a talker, my dad. He just said, 'Ah,' and nodded kind of thoughtfully, then went back to his book."

Even with only that brief meeting with Adam's dad to go on, I have no trouble picturing his reaction. I lay down the grater with a sigh. "You're so lucky."

"Why? You think your parents will mind?" Adam reduces the heat under the pans and turns to me, hip resting against the worktop.

I shake my head. "Not mind as such. It isn't like they're homophobic or anything. I'm sure it'll worry them, though."

"They think you'll get bullied?"

"I suppose so. My dad had a terrible time of it at school. Even back then, he was way more into baking cupcakes than kicking a ball around, so that automatically meant he was gay."

"Whereas we're in the first eleven of our school football teams, so we must be straight. Life's messed up sometimes. How about your mum?"

I meet his gaze, my mouth twitching in a sheepish smile. "Oh, she'd worry whatever. It's what she does."

"Figures." Adam grins at me, his tone teasing, though his eyes are soft. He hooks his fingers into the waistband of my jeans, drawing me against him, and kisses me.

THURSDAY SEES A lull in the relentless rain, and the sun finally makes an appearance. After loading our bikes into the back of Adam's car, we drive to Brookminster Beeches on the outskirts of the city. We cycle through the trees, along twisting pathways dappled russet and amber in the morning light, Adam in the lead, me hot on his wheels. It's a perfect autumn day, the air crisp and cold and flavoured with the smoky tang of bonfires. A breeze whips our hair back from our faces, stealing the words we call out to each other as we weave between small children on scooters and dogs taking their owners for a walk.

At the little café, I buy us hot chocolates and we wander a short way from the packed picnic tables to sit on a bench beneath a beech tree, our bikes leaning against the trunk.

I wrap my numb hands around the polystyrene cup to warm them and grimace at Adam. "Sorry about this evening."

My parents, understandably curious about the boy I've been spending all my free time with, asked me to invite Adam for dinner. I'd been afraid he'd balk at the prospect of meeting my family so soon, but I should have known better.

"Really," Adam says with his easy smile, "it's fine. I'd have to be an idiot to turn down the chance to try some more of your dad's baking."

I laugh, though uncertainty continues to gnaw at me. I stare up at the branches overhead, draped in their holey blanket of brown and gold leaves. "And are you sure you're OK with, you know, not telling my parents?"

"Course." Adam leans in, his shoulder brushing my own. "Like I said before, no one else gets to decide when you come out. You have to be ready."

Reassured, I let out my breath. His shoulder presses into mine, solid, dependable. I want to melt into the contact, to accept the comfort it offers. Instead, I shift away from him, breaking the connection, and scan the trees for potential observers. To cover the movement, I take a gulp of hot chocolate and scald my tongue. Adam watches me, his eyes sympathetic, and guilt leaves a bitter taste in my mouth.

"Sorry," I say again, flushing. "I'm rubbish."

"Nah, not rubbish. You're new to all this, that's all."

Adam grins at me in that infectious way of his that has me grinning back, despite myself. I take another sip of hot chocolate. It's watery and coats my tongue with a fine powder but thaws me right through.

"This isn't so new to you, is it?" I've wondered about it before, about previous boyfriends, but was too wrapped up in the present to dwell on the past.

He shrugs, kicking up a flurry of leaves with the toe of his trainer. "Not so much, but I'm hardly a veteran."

"You've had boyfriends, though?"

"One…kind of. I thought so, anyway."

I study Adam's expression, detecting a tightness I haven't seen in it before. "What happened?"

"He was in denial. Michael and me, we were best mates from our first day at high school. I always had a bit of a thing for him but accepted it would never go anywhere. Then, when we were fourteen, we were lying on my bed one weekend listening to music and, out of nowhere, he kissed me. I was like…wow. It was as if all my wet dreams had come true. I thought that was it, that Michael was my boyfriend, but then the next day, he acted as though the kiss hadn't happened."

"Ouch."

"Yeah, well, that's how it was with us. We'd fool around whenever Michael was in the mood, and then he'd go back to pretending we were just mates. The few times I tried to have it out with him, he shut me down. He wasn't gay, he said. We were just getting each other off. It didn't mean anything."

I wince. Adam's tone is matter-of-fact, but he can't keep the hurt from seeping through. "How long were you…?"

"Three years. In the end, I couldn't take it anymore. I told Michael he had to admit what was between us, if only to himself, or we were done. That was that. We avoided each other for the rest of the year. I couldn't face going back to school after the summer, not when we were taking most of the same subjects. Plus, things had been strained between my stepdad and me for a while, so I decided to come and live with Dad and finish my A' Levels at Brookminster Grammar. Michael and I haven't spoken since."

As Adam talks, a sick feeling settles in the pit of my stomach. He always seems so confident, so unshakable; I never would have guessed what he's been through. My heart aches for him. The realisation that his so-called boyfriend was prepared to throw away their relationship rather than be honest with himself must have been painful enough, but to have lost his best mate as well… Now, here I am, behaving every bit as selfishly as Michael, forcing Adam to keep what we have a secret because I'm scared of how people might react.

Adam bumps my knee with his. "I know what you're thinking, and it isn't true."

"Isn't it?" I stare down into my cup, avoiding his gaze.

"Davey, you know who you are. You aren't trying to delude yourself you're anything you're not. You…need some time, that's all."

I dart him a shy smile. I hope he's right. Adam has been hurt so much already, the last thing in the world I want to do is cause him any more pain.

CHAPTER NINE

"D on't forget." My sister's voice pursues us along the hall. "Nacho Cheese Doritos and the biggest bag of Skittles you can find."

I pull the door to the flat shut behind us and roll my eyes at Adam. "Sorry. Elle's a pain."

"She's your sister," Adam says, as though this explains everything, but there's a wistfulness beneath his amusement.

As we start down the stairs, I ask, "You miss not having your sisters around?"

"Sometimes. Not that they can't be right pains in the arse, but they're a lot younger than Elle so they kind of look up to me. I like that."

"Yeah, that must be nice." I try to imagine a situation in which my sister might view me with anything other than exasperated incomprehension, and fail utterly.

"Aw, Elle looks up to you in her own way, trust me."

"Only because she's five foot nothing."

Adam laughs, his arm pressing into mine, and happiness blooms in my chest. I love that I can make him laugh.

The tension I'd been storing up all day evaporates. Throughout dinner, while Adam charmed my parents as I'd known he would, I was braced for the bullet to fire—for Mum to ask, 'So, Adam, is there anyone special in your life at the moment?'; for Adam to let slip about us being more than friends; for my family to look between us and just know, because surely this thing we have must be visible for all to see.

As usual, my worries amounted to nothing. So far, the evening has gone better than I dared hope. My family absorbed Adam into the Tomkins clan as though him being there was no big deal, as though I have friends over for dinner every night of the week. Dad did his best to talk football with him, his cluelessness making the effort all the more endearing, while Mum insisted Adam eat second helpings of spaghetti bolognese and Elle fluttered her eyelashes at him across the table—her way of showing she approves.

If I'd been in any doubt that my boyfriend—God, I actually have a boyfriend—would be embraced with open arms, these were well and truly dispelled when Elle asked if he could stay for our weekly movie night, and my parents behaved as though this had been the plan all along.

Our tradition of gathering in front of the telly after dinner on a Thursday goes back as far as I can remember. The four of us take it in turns to pick the film, and once the washing up has been done, we assemble in the living room: Dad in his favourite armchair; Mum squashed between Elle and me on the sofa. Around mouthfuls of popcorn and crisps, we discuss the action on screen, Elle and me bemoaning our parents' choices while secretly enjoying them. No one but Gemma, Elle's best friend since playgroup, has ever been allowed to participate... until tonight.

It means the world to me, knowing my family understands what so drew me to Adam, that they feel it too. Yet, my unease lingers, pinching my gut. Would they have taken to him with such wholehearted enthusiasm if they knew the truth?

In the rear hallway, torrential rain splatters against the small windows, the morning's sunshine a distant memory. When I open the back door, wind hurls icy pellets into our faces and we grimace at each other.

"Last one to the car is a steaming dog poo," Adam says, and sprints across the car park.

He's fast, but so am I. I fling myself after him, feet pounding the concrete, both of us giggling as we splash through puddles, drenching the hems of our jeans. Adam reaches the car a millisecond before I do, then fumbles his keys, which land with a splosh on the ground.

"Nice one, Joe Hart." I bend to retrieve them, handing them to Adam with a grin.

He takes the keys, his smile rueful. "And that, I'm afraid, is why I'm a striker rather than a goalie."

I laugh, hurrying around to the passenger side. The moment the lock clicks, we tumble into the front seats, soaking wet and breathless. Adam starts the engine, cranking the heat as high as it can go, but makes no move to pull out of the car park. We're silent for a while, sitting there in the dark interior of Adam's Vauxhall, listening to the rain hammer on the roof. For something to do, I doodle in the condensation on the window with a finger.

"Davey?" Adam waits for me to glance over at him, then says, "Thanks."

"For what?"

"For tonight. For inviting me."

"Come off it. I'm sure watching a film with my parents isn't the most exciting way you could have spent your evening."

"Seriously, your family's cool."

I smile at him, hoping he can read the gratitude in my expression. His eyes meet mine, holding them. All at once, I'm aware how close we are, nothing but the gear stick between us, and that this is the first time we've been properly alone all day. The need to kiss him, to fist my fingers in his hair and feel his mouth on mine, sparks a physical ache in my groin, in my heart.

I tear my gaze away and stare through the windscreen. Adam touches my leg, squeezing once to show he understands, then reverses out of the parking space. I wish I were brave enough to kiss Adam in full view of anyone who might stroll by, to kiss him and not give a damn who sees. One day, I hope I will be, but not yet.

It's surreal, walking into Pardo's with Adam. The aisles are mostly empty this near to closing time, and the fluorescent lighting dazzles me after the darkness outside. Though we're in public, the absence of other shoppers creates the illusion that we're in our own little bubble, protected, untouchable.

As we head for the dairy aisle, Adam bumps my shoulder with his, and our gazes brush. An image pops into my mind—the two of us a few years from now, our togetherness obvious in our familiarity, the easy way we argue over whether to go for Indian or Chinese. Shopping done, we'll return to the cosy apartment we've made our own, where we'll open a bottle of wine and eat dinner in front of the latest episode of *Doctor Who*. It's stupid, a fantasy. All the same, the possibility of it pulls my mouth into a grin. Adam catches my mood and grins back. It could happen, if we wanted it to. We could make this thing work.

We arrive in the dairy section to find the shelves devoid of semi-skimmed milk. I curse, scanning the few remaining bottles in the hope that one might be hiding amidst the skimmed and full fat.

Adam nudges me and points to the end of the aisle, where a woman in a Pardo's uniform is passing. "You go and get the snacks and I'll ask about the milk. Meet you at the checkouts?"

"Right." I give him the thumbs up and head back towards the front of the store.

I've filled my arms with crisps and chocolate bars and am searching the shelves for the largest bag of Skittles on offer, when a horribly familiar voice sounds behind me.

"Davey, yo!"

The ensuing clap on the back almost sends me face first into a display of Haribo. *Shit.* My heart drops to the shiny vinyl floor. *Shit, shit, shit.* I turn, snacks sliding in my grasp, to find Kyle grinning at me.

"Goalkeeper to the rescue." He steadies the packet of Doritos in my arms before it can slip from the top of the pile. "You been sent out on errand duty, too?"

"Sorry?" I look at him, unable to comprehend him over the terror pounding in my ears. Of all my teammates I could have run into, why did it have to be Kyle Matthews? If Adam shows up now…

"Errand duty," Kyle repeats, emphasising each syllable as though speaking to someone who doesn't understand English. He holds up a tin of tomatoes to illustrate his point.

"Oh, right. Yeah." I cringe, cheeks flaming. *Hold it together, Davey. He mustn't suspect anything's up.* "So, um, good half-term?"

The moment the question spills out, I want nothing more than to gnaw through my own vocal cords. *Nice one, genius.*

What better way to get rid of him as quickly as possible than starting a conversation? Sweat prickles my palms, and I clutch my goodies more tightly to my chest in an attempt to hide the fact that I'm shaking. Kyle launches into a description of his and Stu's *Call of Duty* marathon, but the words become garbled en route to my brain. Gaze skittering from one end of the store to the other, scanning the entrances to the aisles, I will Adam to somehow sense my panic, pray he'll read my mental distress signals and steer clear.

So much for that.

Kyle's in full flow, describing a particularly intense battle, when Adam rounds the corner and makes straight for us. He holds up a bottle of milk, his grin triumphant. I widen my eyes, trying to warn him without attracting Kyle's attention. The first part works because Adam stops in his tracks, smile fading. However, my alarm also alerts Kyle, who pauses mid-sentence to glance over his shoulder.

"Look who it is." His lips curl in a sneer. "Bit out of your way, aren't you, fag boy? Here visiting your boyfriend?"

I wince, but Adam seems unperturbed. He raises an eyebrow at Kyle, expression neutral.

"What the hell's he doing here?" Kyle turns to me, face twisted with contempt. "It's bad enough we have to play against the poofter, without running into him on our doorstep."

I open my mouth, knowing I have to defend Adam. *Don't call him that*, I should say. *He's with me, so keep your filthy opinions to yourself.* Instead, I merely shrug. "I have no idea."

The denial tastes bitter on my tongue, the taste of shame. Sickened with myself, I turn my back on Adam, but not before I see the hurt that flickers in his eyes.

CHAPTER TEN

"FINALLY! WHAT TOOK you so…" Elle skids to a stop in the hallway, eyes widening. "Wow, what happened to you?"

I stare at her through a curtain of numbness, sopping hair plastered to my forehead. Water drips from my clothes and pools on the carpet.

"Davey?" Mum appears in the doorway to the living room. When she sees me, her hand flies to her mouth and she hurries to my side. "Davey, you're soaked. Are you OK? I was starting to worry. Where's Adam?"

"He's gone." The words come out flat and hollow—the same words that haunted me, chanting in time with the downpour, all through the interminable walk home.

I can't get it out of my head—the way Adam looked, his expression of naked hurt, before he turned from me and left. Somehow, I kept it together as I paid and said goodbye to Kyle, stalling by the newspaper stand to give him the chance to drive off. By the time I made it out into the car park, the space where Adam's Vauxhall had been was empty.

"Gone?" Mum repeats, confusion evident in her voice. "Where? Why? Don't tell me you walked all the way from Pardo's in the rain. Davey, look at me."

Gentle hands grasp my shoulders. I can't look at Mum, can't face the concern reflected in her tone. A peep from beneath my lashes shows her brow creased with worry, and Elle at Mum's elbow, chewing on her lip. My gaze fixes on my sodden trainers. I don't deserve their concern. If they knew what I'd done, how I'd treated Adam, they'd be disgusted, although nowhere near as disgusted as I am with myself.

"He wasn't feeling well." It's a testament to my misery that I barely trip over the lie. "I told him to drop me at the end of the road and get home."

Without glancing up, I can feel Elle's scrutiny like a searchlight. She has a nose to rival a beagle's when it comes to sniffing out bullshit.

"Oh, what a shame." Mum's frown clears before her gaze narrows on me. "You look a little peaky, too. Perhaps you're coming down with whatever Adam has. Go and take those wet clothes off and get into bed, and I'll bring you a hot drink."

I duck past her, unable to meet her eye. I hate lying to my mum. Guilt, as cloying and viscous as tar, joins the shame over Adam already clogging my throat. It would serve me right if I suffocated on it.

"Here," I mutter, shoving the carrier bag of snacks at Elle. "Sorry, Mum, forgot the milk."

Mum gives me a little push. "Don't be silly. Just get yourself in the warm. Go on, before you catch a chill."

I don't have the energy to do anything other than let myself be mothered. As soon as I'm in my room with the door shut, I pull out my phone and call Adam. It goes straight to voicemail. The sound of his voice—warm and familiar with that hint of gravel—boots me in the stomach.

"Adam, it's me." My own voice cracks. "I'm so sorry. Please call back, let me explain. I never meant… Please."

Before I can break down, I hang up and toss the phone onto the bedside cabinet. Then I strip off my drenched clothes and crawl into bed, pulling the duvet over my head in an effort to block out the world.

Adam doesn't call back. He doesn't reply to any of my texts, nor does he pick up on the few occasions I pluck up the courage to dial his number. I don't blame him; I wouldn't want to talk to me either. All the same, I wish he'd at least hear me out.

Mum, certain I'm suffering from the same illness as Adam, insists I take it easy for the next couple of days, and I don't argue. With the persistent pounding in my head and my stomach so knotted with misery and regret that I feel constantly on the verge of throwing up, it's a relief to have an excuse to be alone. I huddle on my side under the covers, alternately losing myself in fitful sleep and enduring the torture of my own thoughts. I curse Kyle for appearing when he did, for bursting our private bubble—curse my own inability to look him in the eye and tell the truth. Sometimes I curse Adam for refusing to speak to me, denying me the opportunity to explain. Hadn't he, after all, made it clear that the choice to come out should be mine and mine alone?

When Sunday afternoon comes and there's still no word from Adam, I can't stand it any longer. I have a hot shower, pull on my comfiest sweatshirt and tracksuit bottoms, and head downstairs to let my parents know I'm going out. If Adam won't answer his phone, I'll have to talk to him face-to-face.

During the drive to Brookminster, I marvel at how composed I am, the steadiness of my hands on the steering wheel. It's as though my brain has worn itself out with its ceaseless circling, and now I've made the decision to act, my mind is still and crystal clear. Adam may want nothing more to do with me, but I can't let him walk out of my life without apologising to him in person.

Unlike my first visit to Adam's—was it really only a week ago?—this time I don't hesitate. After pulling into a spot in the car park, I get out of the car and cross the road to the apartment block, where I jab my finger on the buzzer. There's a few moments of silence, then a click.

"Hello?" Even over the crackle, his voice sounds tired and empty of its usual animation.

"Adam, it's me."

He's quiet for so long I'm afraid he'll hang up without letting me in, but at last he says, "Wait there."

He's gone before I can respond. It strikes me as a dubious sign that he's coming down to meet me rather than inviting me up, but I'll take whatever scraps I can salvage. I bury my hands in my coat pockets and gaze out along the road. Except for the occasional passing car, everywhere is quiet, the afternoon windless and grey. A minute or so later, the door swings open and Adam steps onto the porch, pulling it shut behind him.

"Hey." He doesn't look at me, intent on zipping up his leather jacket, and his tone still holds that curious listlessness.

"Hey." My heart accelerates at the sight of him, at the warmth radiating from his body, the faint suggestion of that clean, woody scent. I want nothing more than to push him up against the wall and kiss the breath from his lungs, to have his arms come around me, anchoring me close, to feel him, taste him. But I can't. Perhaps, if I'm lucky, that will come later. Before then, I have to earn his forgiveness.

"Come on." Without glancing my way, Adam gestures for me to follow him, and we walk a short distance along the street. There, he leans against the brick wall and fishes a packet of Sovereigns from his coat pocket.

I stare, jolted from my nerves. "I didn't know you smoked."

"Used to." Adam extracts a cigarette and ignites it with a practised flick of a lighter, "but it played havoc with my fitness so I gave up."

And now he's smoking again, risking his performance on the pitch, all because of me, my betrayal. Fresh remorse swamps me.

"I'm sorry." The words tumble out of me in an untidy rush. "God, Adam, I can't tell you how sorry I am."

He inhales a lungful of smoke, then releases it on a long sigh. "Don't be."

I blink. I'd been prepared for anger, for accusations fuelled by hurt. I don't know what to do with this calm acceptance.

"I get it, Davey," Adam says. "Seriously. What happened at Pardo's, I should've expected it. Hell, I did expect it."

My shoulders sag, a little of the tension sliding away, and I lean against the wall, half turned towards him. "Then why? Why wouldn't you talk to me?"

"Needed time, I suppose. I needed to think, to work out how I feel about it."

"And how do you feel?"

Adam looks at me then. Even through the gloom, I can make out the sadness in his eyes, the dark shadows beneath them. "I'm sorry, Davey. I don't think I can do this."

"But…" My momentary relief fades, dread settling like cold cement in my gut. "You said you understood."

"This isn't about you. It's me."

I bite my lip. I'd envisaged so many ways this conversation might go, but in none of my imaginings had it gone anything like this. I'd come here intending to say so much, but it seems Adam's the one who needs to talk.

He sucks in another mouthful of smoke, his glowing cigarette end the only bright spot in the approaching dusk. "I can't do this again, not after Michael. I can't be someone's secret, your secret. I thought I could, but I can't. I'm sorry."

Tears sting my eyelids and I clench my fists, willing them not to fall. Nevertheless, my voice breaks. "You won't have to. I can do it…come out."

Adam shakes his head. "No, you can't. You're not ready. However much I might wish you were, you're not."

I want to argue with him, to assure him I am ready, that I'll do whatever he needs me to, so long as he'll give me another chance. But I don't. I don't because, in my heart, I know he's right.

"Don't think this is easy for me." For the first time that afternoon, Adam's cool fractures, his words trembling. "If you knew how fucking hard this is…but I have to. If I were to keep seeing you, I'd end up putting pressure on you, pushing you into something before you're ready, and I can't do that. I…I like you too much."

I bow my head in defeat. My insides feel empty, hollowed out. A single tear trickles from beneath my lashes and carves a hot trail down my cheek. I swallow. "That's it, then?"

"Yeah." Adam drops his cigarette to the pavement and crushes it underfoot, along with my last fragment of hope. "I think it is."

CHAPTER ELEVEN

I RETURN TO SCHOOL after the half-term break in a daze. If I were viewing myself from the perspective of a casual observer, it would seem as though nothing has changed. I keep my head down in class, hand in my homework on time and perform on the pitch with my usual quiet focus. Yet, however hard I try to immerse myself in the everyday routine, I can't shift the weight of unhappiness and regret dragging at my heart.

Had this really been my life only a few short weeks ago? How had I stood it, this monotony of essays and equations, this hiding away and fearing to be myself? From the afternoon of the tournament, when my eyes met Adam's across the field, I'd felt truly alive for the first time in years. Those hours we'd spent together this past week had been incredible, game-changing, like coming round after a coma that stole my adolescence. I'd discovered how it felt to be accepted for all my quirks and idiosyncrasies, and not just accepted: liked. I'd experienced the rush of having Adam's mouth on mine, his muscular hardness pressing me into the bed, the intake of breath that told me he was every bit as turned on as I was.

And I threw it all away.

"Good job, lads," Mr. Barry calls as we make our way off the field at the end of practice on the second Thursday after half-term. "Play like that on Sunday and we'll have no problem against the Buzzards."

My toe catches on an uneven patch of ground and I stumble. Shock sends my head into a spin. How, during the previous training sessions, could I have failed to register the fact that our next match is against Adam's team? I'd known, of course, that we'd be coming up against them at some point in the season; I just hadn't expected it to be so soon.

"And, Davey," Mr. Barry's hand lands on my shoulder, "do try not to break anyone's leg this time, eh?"

The others hoot with laughter, but I'm too embroiled in my own panic to be embarrassed. I allow myself to be jostled inside amidst my sweat-soaked teammates, all hurrying to get out of the cold. In the changing room, I sink onto the bench in front of my locker and fumble with my bootlaces, deaf to the chatter around me. There's no way I can play on Sunday—no way I can face him after what I did. Still, even as my fingers tingle and the blood thrums in my ears, the prospect of seeing him again sets me alight with anticipation.

"Hey." Jermain drops onto the bench beside me, already changed back into his school uniform. How long have I been sitting here?

"Hey." Finally managing to untie my laces, I concentrate on pulling off my muddy boots as an excuse to avoid his steady gaze.

"Tell me to butt out," Jermain says, "but you've been really quiet lately. Quieter than normal, I mean. Something up?"

Before I can begin to think how to respond, Kyle jumps in. "Obvious, isn't it?"

His words douse me in icy perspiration. It erupts on my palms, my forehead, under my arms, down my spine. The boot slips from my grasp and falls to the tiled floor with a *thunk*.

He knows. Despite my misguided efforts to cover my tracks, Kyle has added it all up and come to the only answer that makes sense. Why, though, has he waited until now to say something?

Kyle grimaces at me. "Did she dump you, then, that bird you were shagging?"

I slump against my locker, but even as relief overwhelms the anxiety, I suppress a wince. Although his shot sailed wide of goal, it came close enough to hurt.

"Aw." Partway through buttoning his shirt, Jimmy shakes his head. "Cheer up, Davey. There're plenty more where she came from."

"Yeah, she's not worth it." Jermain squeezes my shoulder, his smile kind.

I gaze around at my fellow Falcons, at their identical expressions of sympathy. This camaraderie, this sense of belonging, is what it has all been about. I'd sacrificed my growing relationship with Adam so that I could hold onto my teammates' respect. Because of my betrayal I'm still part of the team, but at what cost? Not a single person in this room knows the real me.

'Being popular doesn't mean much when nobody knows who you really are,' Adam had said during our first proper conversation, the evening I left school after training to find him there, waiting for me.

I'd always considered it a fair price to pay, keeping so much of myself locked away in return for being accepted, but if that acceptance is no longer making me happy, where's the point in any of it?

HEART POUNDING, HARDLY aware of what I'm doing, I reach for the clean bowl Dad has just set on the drainer. My fingers, clumsy with nerves, slip on the smooth surface.

"Whoa there!" Dad rescues the bowl from my grasp and places it on the worktop, then rests a hand on my shoulder. It's still wet and soapy from the washing-up water, and the dampness seeps through my sweatshirt. I look up to find his concerned gaze on me. "What is it? You've been jittery all evening."

I twist the tea towel around and around in my fists, coiling it into a rope. The decision that seemed so clear-cut in the changing room that afternoon rears above me, dark and fraught with peril, impossible to scale. All through dinner, I'd pushed my cottage pie around with my fork, seeking the right words to say what I needed to. Even now that it's just Dad and me in the kitchen, I'm no nearer working out where to start.

Dad gives my shoulder a reassuring pat. "You can tell me anything. You know that, don't you?"

I grip the tea towel until my knuckles are in danger of punching through the skin. How can I tell him? How can I look my kind, sensitive father in the eye and tell him something that will carve lines of anxiety into his face? How can I knowingly do that to him and to my mum? Yet, how can I not?

"Feel free to tell me to mind my own business," Dad says, speaking with obvious care, "but does it have anything to do with Adam?"

My heart thuds painfully at the sound of his name. The familiar panic seizes hold of me, though this time it's mingled with hope. Perhaps Dad has already guessed. Well, it wouldn't be hard to figure out. For a short time, Adam had been the centre of my small world, consuming my every spare moment. Then, without warning, he was gone, and beyond Mum's tentative enquiry as to when I might be seeing him next, my family has barely mentioned his absence. Even Elle has passed up the opportunity to comment on my inability to hold onto a single friend. I'd been too wrapped up in my own wretchedness to notice their reticence before, but now it strikes me as odd.

"It's just that you seemed different when Adam was here," Dad says. "Happier, I suppose. It was nice to see."

He pats my shoulder once more and returns to the washing up. He's always been good at judging when I'm ready to talk—when to push, and when to let me work up to it in my own time.

I smooth the creases from the tea towel and reach for the next bowl, handling it with exaggerated caution. A concrete slab has lodged itself in my stomach. I'm not going to do it. Despite my good intentions, I'm about to let this chance slip away. Soon, the dishes will be done. Dad and I will go through to the living room where the four of us will settle in our usual seats to watch the film—Mum's choice this week—and life will continue as normal. The truth will fester inside me like an untreated wound, poisoning my relationship with everyone I care about, and all because I'm too much of a coward to say those few simple words.

"You know," Dad says, his voice conversational, "you could try talking to him. To Adam. Whatever went wrong between you—"

"I'm gay." The admission bursts from me, far louder than I'd meant it to. It's as though a surgeon has plunged a scalpel into that festering wound, releasing the pus in a stream of agony and relief.

Dad blinks, clearly taken aback. He removes the tea towel from my unresisting fingers and dries his hands, his movements slow, measured. Unable to confront his reaction when it comes, I bury my face in my arms.

"I'm gay." This time I speak the words more to myself than to him, my voice scarcely above a croak.

A snort comes from behind me, and I jerk my head around to find Elle poised in the doorway to the hall.

"And now, ladies and gentlemen," she says as though addressing an invisible audience, "we have a breaking announcement. My brother, the star footballer who has never so much as looked at a girl in his life, is gay, something which will come as a shock to precisely no one."

"Elle…" Dad's tone carries a warning.

I look from one of them to the other, sure I'm missing something, that Elle can't mean what I think she does.

"What?" Elle waltzes over to the fridge and opens it, snagging a Coke. "Oh, sorry, was I supposed to act all surprised, like Davey coming out is the biggest shock of the century?"

"Danielle!" Dad raises his voice, something he rarely does, and Elle's mouth snaps shut on her retort. With a pout, she pops the ring pull on her can and saunters into the hall.

I turn to Dad, disbelief and hope swelling to fill my chest. "You knew?"

"We…suspected." Dad's smile is soft, full of compassion. He lays a hand on my back, guiding me over to the table and into a chair.

"But…" I sink onto it, struggling to assimilate this information. "Why didn't you say anything?"

"Your mum and I didn't want to assume." Dad lowers himself into the chair next to me, his hand still on my back. "We were waiting for you to come to us."

"I wanted to, really I did, but I didn't want to worry you. More than I do already, I mean."

Dad lets out a rueful chuckle. "Worrying is par for the course when you're a parent, I'm afraid. We'd rather you talked to us instead of keeping everything bottled up. All we want, all we've ever wanted, is for you to be happy."

Relief, warm and comforting as a goose-down duvet on a cold night, settles around me. I rest my elbows on the table, cradling my chin in my hands. I've done it. I've come out to my dad—and to Elle, too, albeit unwittingly—and nothing terrible has happened. They weren't even surprised, as it turns out.

"About Adam," Dad says. "Was he more than a friend to you?"

I nod, swallowing against the sudden lump in my throat. "But I messed up, Dad. I really messed up."

I tell him how I met Adam at the football tournament earlier in the season, about my fear of my teammates discovering I'm gay, and how I'd wanted to see him anyway. I explain about Michael, the boy who broke Adam's heart, and what I'd done when we met Kyle in the supermarket the night Adam came for dinner, how I'd betrayed him.

Dad nods when I've finished, looking pensive. "It seems to me that you and Adam might have something special, something that's worth fighting for."

I manage a weak smile, more grateful than I could ever express to have my dad here with me, on my side. "I think so, too, but how?"

Even as I ask the question, the answer begins to form in my mind. It's obvious, really. I could try talking to him again, but words wouldn't be enough. I need to prove to him, beyond any shadow of a doubt, that I won't let him down a second time. All at once, I know exactly what I have to do.

CHAPTER TWELVE

I REST MY CHEEK against the window of the school minibus and stare out at the all too familiar road to Brookminster. It's a perfect autumn morning, pale shafts of sunshine warming my skin—so different from that day earlier in the season when my eyes first met Adam's, the day that changed everything. Adam broke through the defensive wall I'd erected around myself, dismantling it brick by painstakingly laid brick, until I no longer have any idea how to repair the damage or if I even want to.

The usual pre-match rowdiness fills the bus, but I'm too focused on keeping down my breakfast to pay much attention. In less than an hour, I'll see him. My stomach aches from curling itself into a protective ball. I know what I have to do, just not whether I have the courage to go through with it. And even if I have, what if I've already blown it? Chances are, he'll want nothing more to do with me, and who could blame him?

"All right?" Jermain nudges me with his massive shoulder.

I nod, not trusting myself to speak.

Kyle leans forward, resting his elbows on the back of our seat. "Not worrying about that homo, are you, Davey?"

From beside him, Stu lets out a soft snort.

My insides go still. Slowly, I twist to face him. "I'm sorry?"

"Seriously," Kyle punches me on the arm, "don't sweat it. You're more than a match for that pansy."

Heat rushes to my face. It's a moment before I realise the flush stems from anger rather than embarrassment. This knowledge lends me strength and I take a deep breath. "Cut it out." My voice, quieter than I intend, cracks with nerves.

Kyle frowns in evident confusion. "What did you say?"

"I said cut it out. What's Adam ever done to you?" This time, my words come out loud and clear, setting off a chorus of cheers and catcalls.

"That told you, mate." Jimmy smirks. "Good on you, Davey."

Kyle shoots me a filthy look and flops back in his seat. "Only trying to help. I won't bother in future."

Jermain winks at me, his smile surprised but not unfriendly. In fact, other than Kyle, no one seems put out by my defence of Adam, merely entertained. They go back to discussing their plans for that afternoon and I return to gazing out of the window, my pulse racing.

I'M WALKING ONTO the football pitch with the rest of my team when I see him.

I slow to a halt, the ground firm beneath my boots, and squint through the sun. At the sight of him, my heart slams against my ribs. Even surrounded by his teammates, all decked out in their royal-blue and yellow, he draws my gaze. Adam isn't looking at me. If anything, I'd say he's making a concerted effort to avoid so much as glancing in my direction. He's unusually still, stiller than I've ever seen him. It's as if all the pent-up energy—one of the first things I noticed about him—has been buried so deep that it can no longer find its way to the surface. He simply stands there, thumbs hooked into the waistband of his shorts, listening to his coach with quiet intensity.

The change in him is painful to see, and remorse deals me a blow to the stomach. I never wanted to hurt him like this. Yet it gives me hope, too—hope that Adam might be missing me every bit as much as I've missed him. Perhaps, as I've scarcely allowed myself to believe, there's still a chance for us.

Mr. Barry launches into his pep talk, but my mind is elsewhere, fixated on what I have to do. Anxiety sets my fingers tingling and my breathing comes hard and fast. I take a few moments to get myself under control.

Inhale…hold…release.

Inhale…hold…release.

As if in a dream, on legs as insubstantial as wet clay, I step away from the Falcons and begin crossing the pitch.

"Oy, Tomkins!" Coach's indignation pursues me. "Where do you think you're off to?"

Several of my teammates snigger, and Kyle says in a tone clearly meant to carry, "Looks like Davey's decided to play for the other team."

My cheeks grow hot, but I ignore my coach's question and Kyle's blatant insinuation. With my gaze trained on the far touchline, I force myself to move forward, placing one foot in front of the other. This must have been how it felt to be a condemned prisoner in the Middle Ages, walking the final path from a cell in the Tower of London to meet his death on the scaffold, the distance seeming somehow both interminable and far too short.

Adam, along with several of his fellow Buzzards, turns to stare at me, following my deliberate progress towards him. His eyes, wide with amazement and uncertainty, snag mine, and I lock onto them. My vision contracts, blocking out everything but Adam's face, homing in on it as though on a single lighted window amidst a sea of densest fog, until I'm within a metre of him.

"Davey..." Like me, Adam seems to be having trouble believing I'm really here, in view of everyone, close enough for him to reach out and touch. "What—?"

Before my brain can list all the reasons why this is a terrible idea, I lean in and kiss him. Adam doesn't respond; his lips remain cool and immobile beneath mine. Humiliation, blistering as a bucket of scalding water, douses me from scalp to toe. I'm too late. I had my opportunity and I threw it away. Now I've laid myself bare, exposed the most secret part of my heart for everyone to see, and all for nothing.

I'm about to jerk away when Adam returns my kiss with a hunger that has me stumbling backwards. His hands come up to grip my shoulders, his fingers burning through my shirt, and my arms go around him, as much to steady myself as to pull Adam closer. We simply stand there, holding onto each other, kissing on and on. Everything around us fades. I'm aware of nothing but the warmth of Adam's mouth on mine, the teasing caress of his tongue, the delicious taste of him.

When we eventually come up for air, Adam exhales a shaky breath. "Wow."

With the suddenness of a TV being unmuted, sound roars to life around us. I feel light-headed, dizzy, as though I've stepped off the Merry Mixer at the annual steam fair. All at once, I'm conscious of the shouts and wolf whistles from our respective teammates. I tear my gaze from Adam's and risk a glance at the Falcons. I'm in time to see the rage and disgust contorting Kyle's features, before he presents his back to me and stalks away. Stu merely offers me a shrug and follows his friend.

With a plunging sensation in my belly, I scan the rest of my team. Jermain gives me the thumbs up and Jimmy's face is split in a grin. Though there are several raised eyebrows and a good deal of muttering, no one looks revolted or displeased. As I stand there, stunned by what I've done, Jimmy starts to clap. Jermain joins in, and soon the whole lot of them are clapping and cheering and stamping their feet…for me.

I return my attention to Adam. He's smiling at me, his eyes full of wonder and more brilliant than I've ever seen them. I smile back, my heart ballooning with happiness and pride, excitement and terror, and too many other emotions to catalogue. I've done it. I've come out in front of my entire team and my life hasn't imploded. More importantly, I've proved to Adam—as well as to myself—that I'm ready to show the world who I truly am, to be the person he needs me to be.

"I hope," Adam says, mouth quirking, "that wasn't an attempt to get me to go easy on you, because I'm still going to kick your arse out there."

I laugh. "Go for it."

"Tomkins!" Mr. Barry's voice echoes across the pitch. "I hate to interfere with your love life, but we have a match in five minutes and I need you focused."

"Catch you later?" Adam asks, his gaze on mine.

I nod, my grin unstoppable, and let my fingers brush against his for an instant. Then I turn and cross the field to re-join my squad. I feel weightless, buoyant, supported on a cloud of euphoria at my own daring. There's so much left to say, so much we need to catch up on, but not here, not now. Later, we'll be able to talk and to do all the things we've been starved of these past weeks. We can begin to explore just where our connection—still so fragile and exciting in its newness—might take us.

In the meantime, I have a game to win.

THE END

CLAIM YOUR FREE STORY

Thank you so much for reading. If you enjoyed this book, you can join my readers' club to get a free and exclusive short story in my *Boys on the Brink* series. Simply go to

https://jamiedeacon.com/readersclub

and enter your email address. You'll then receive a welcome email from me with links to download your story in your preferred format.

You'll also be signed up to my newsletter where I share updates on my writing, post giveaways, and generally indulge my passion for the world of YA LGBTQ+ fiction. You can unsubscribe at any time and your data will be kept safe and secure.

Happy reading and I look forward to connecting with you!

Jamie

PLEASE LEAVE A REVIEW

It's no exaggeration to say that, to authors, reviews are invaluable. Just a line or two expressing your thoughts can be such a help in spreading the word to like-minded readers. So, if you enjoyed this book, please consider leaving a review on Amazon or your online bookstore of choice. It would mean more to me than I can say.

ABOUT THE AUTHOR

Jamie Deacon is an award-winning author of young adult LGBTQ+ fiction with a passion for weaving stories about friendship, falling in love and finding the courage to be true to yourself. Their debut novel, *Caught Inside*, won two Rainbow Awards and was nominated for a Lambda Literary Award, a Bisexual Book Award and a Next Generation Indie Book Award.

Jamie was born with Retinitis Pigmentosa, a degenerative eye condition that left them registered blind by their mid-teens. Now only able to view their surroundings in light and shadow, Jamie creates vivid settings inside their head and brings them to life through the magic of words.

Jamie lives with their childhood sweetheart close to the River Thames in Berkshire, England. When not curled under a blanket with a book, they enjoy British comedy, are a huge dog lover, and get way too competitive at family games nights.

To find out more about Jamie and their books, you can visit https://jamiedeacon.com

BOOKS BY JAMIE DEACON

BOYS ON THE BRINK SERIES

Caught Inside
https://jamiedeacon.com/caught-inside

Forbidden Steps
https://jamiedeacon.com/forbidden-steps

Defensive Play (Novella)
https://jamiedeacon.com/defensive-play

Off Course (Short Story)
https://jamiedeacon.com/off-course

STANDALONE TITLES

The Music of Unexpected Things
https://jamiedeacon.com/the-music-of-unexpected-things